LOVE, LEFT UNSAID

A TALE OF UNSPOKEN LOVE BY

AVINASH JAIN

ISBN
Paperback: 979-8-89744-877-7
Hardcase: 979-8-89929-663-5

Some silences deserve their own page

...

For her, for you,
for the stories without endings.

...

ACKNOWLEDGEMENTS

Writing this book was not just about putting words on paper—it was about pouring pieces of my heart into something that would outlive a moment, a memory, or even a person.

To those who loved and lost, who carried feelings too heavy to speak—this book belongs to you.

To my friends and well-wishers, thank you for listening, encouraging, and reminding me that even unspoken love deserves to be written.

To my readers, if even a single line stays with you, this journey was worth it.

And to her—whose five-letter name made me believe in love again, and whose love gave me the strength to finish this story. You are one of the most important reasons this book came to life, and you will always be the most beautiful person in my life.

With gratitude,
Avinash Jain

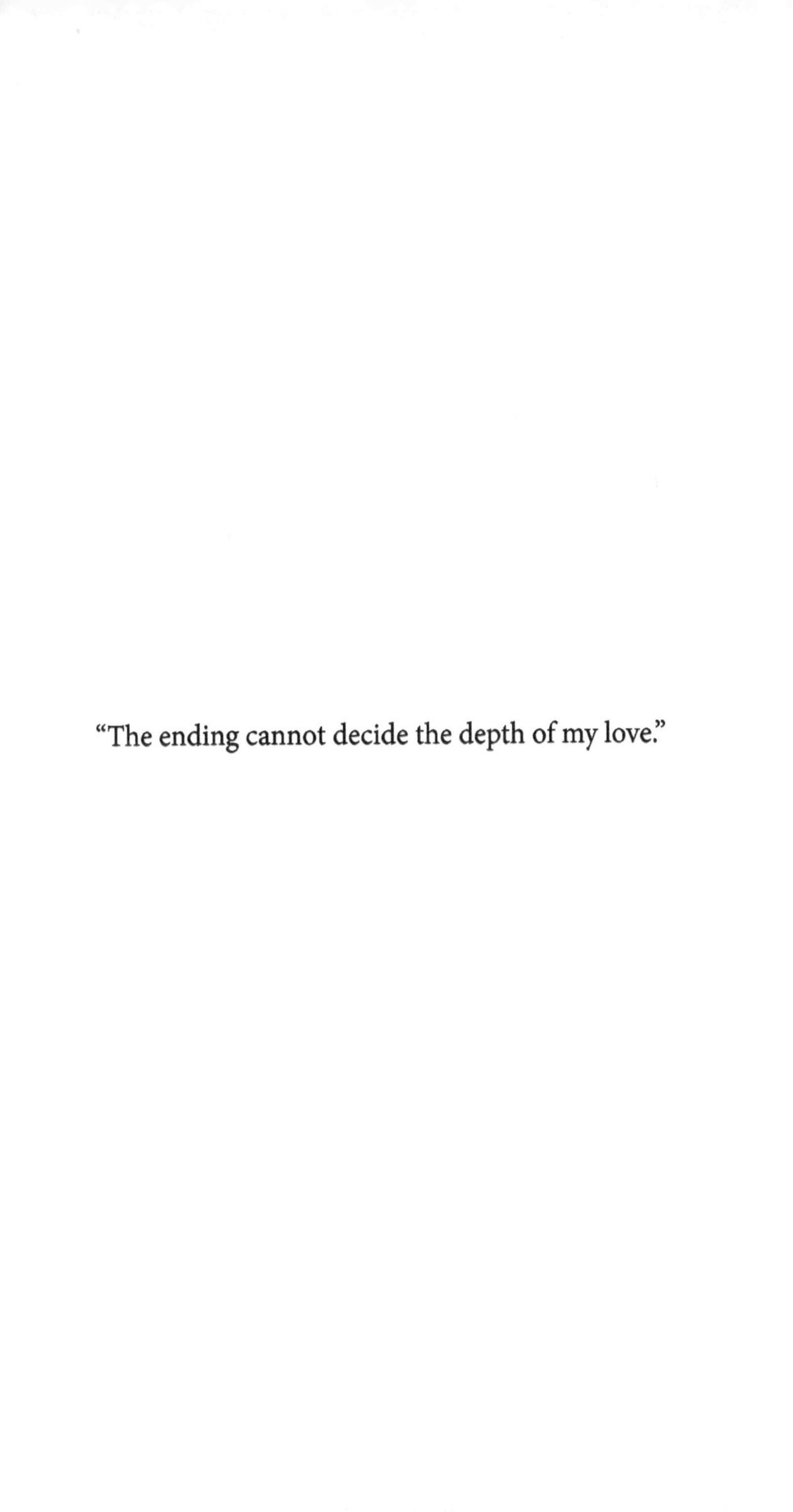

"The ending cannot decide the depth of my love."

FOREWORD

Some love stories are never written with grand beginnings or endings.

They live quietly — between glances, between silences, between the words left unsaid.

Love, Left Unsaid was born from those spaces — from the ache of almosts and the beauty of feelings that had no name.

It is a book stitched together not by perfect stories, but by real ones — the kind that live in the background of our lives and stay long after the moment has passed.

I didn't set out to write a perfect story.

I set out to write an honest one — because some loves don't ask to be celebrated, they ask only to be remembered.

If these pages remind you of someone, of a feeling, of a moment you once held close — then this story was always partly yours too.

Thank you for turning these pages, and for listening to the love I could never say out loud.

With all my heart,

Avinash Jain

CONTENTS

CHAPTER 1

THE WEIGHT OF SILENCE

I don't know when it started.

Maybe it was the first time we met when she smiled at me like I was someone worth knowing. Or perhaps it was somewhere in between—the late-night conversations, the stolen glances, the moments when the world blurred, leaving only her voice behind.

I didn't wake up one day realizing I loved her. It wasn't sudden. It was slow, like a quiet tide creeping up the shore—unnoticed until it was too late.

And by the time I knew it, I was drowning.

I wanted to tell her. God, I wanted to tell her. But every time I thought I'd gathered the courage, something stopped me—fear, hesitation, the gnawing thought that maybe she didn't feel the same. So, I let the words sit at the edge of my tongue, waiting for the right moment.

But the thing about the right moments is that they don't wait for you. They slip past while you hesitate, vanishing before you can reach for them.

I remember one night in particular. We were sitting by the river, the air thick with the scent of earth and distant rain. She was talking, lost in a story about something from her childhood—something funny, something ordinary. But I wasn't listening. Not really.

I was watching her.

The way the wind played with her hair. The way she tucked it behind her ear every few minutes, only for it to fall right back. The way her lips curled when she spoke, how her fingers traced invisible patterns on the fabric of her jeans. Everything about her was effortless, and I was utterly captivated.

She turned to me suddenly, catching me mid-thought.

"What?" she asked, tilting her head, a soft smile teasing her lips.

I opened my mouth. This is it, I thought. Say it.

Tell her that she makes everything feel lighter. Tell her that silence with her is louder than any noise. Tell her that you love her.

But I didn't.

I smiled instead. "Nothing."

She laughed, nudging me playfully before looking away. And just like that, the moment passed.

How many moments had I let slip like that? Too many.

Somewhere deep down, I think she knew. Maybe she saw it in the way I looked at her, in the way my voice softened when I said her name. Maybe she felt it in the pauses between our conversations, in the way my breath hitched when she got too close.

Or maybe she didn't. Maybe she never thought of me that way, and I was just another presence in her life—someone to talk to, to laugh with, to lean on when she needed company.

One evening, we sat on a rooftop, the city flickering below us. The air was cool, carrying the distant hum of life moving on without us. She rested her head on my shoulder, and I let out a breath I didn't realize I had been holding.

I wanted to freeze that moment, to make it stretch a little longer. Because if I couldn't have her the way I wanted, then at least I could have this.

Then, just for a second, she turned to me. Her lips parted like she was about to say something, but she hesitated.

And then she smiled.

Not the kind of smile that said I feel it too.

The kind that said you're important to me, but not in the way you wish you were.

She looked away before I could search her eyes for anything more. And that was it.

I stayed silent, letting my love settle into the space between us, unspoken. Because if silence was the only way I could keep her, then silence it would be.

The world kept moving. Days turned into weeks, weeks into months, and yet, nothing changed. I was still caught in this quiet, aching love—one that lived in lingering glances and unsaid words.

I found myself memorizing the way she existed, the small details that made her who she was. The way she danced when she thought no one was watching. The way she bit her lip when she was lost in thought. The way she held her coffee mug close to her face on cold mornings, as if drawing warmth from more than just the drink inside.

And then there were the moments I wish I could relive—the ones that held me captive long after they had passed.

Like the night she called me at 2 AM, her voice soft and uncertain. "Are you awake?" she asked, though she already knew the answer.

I was always awake for her.

We talked for hours about nothing and everything all at once. And somewhere in between, I almost told her. Almost.

"But almost doesn't count."

She was always just a breath away, just a heartbeat from knowing. And I was always too afraid to bridge the gap.

"Because love like this—love left unsaid—is both a blessing and a curse. It keeps you close, but never close enough. It fills your heart, but never completely."

And it lingers, long after it should have faded.

"Some love exists only in the space between words left unsaid."

CHAPTER 2

THE LOVE THEY NEVER SAW FOR WHAT IT WAS

Love is supposed to be simple, isn't it?

You feel something for someone, you tell them, and either they feel it too, or they don't. But what happens when love exists—real, undeniable—but is never truly seen for what it is?

That's what we were. Something caught between understanding and misinterpretation, lingering in the space where words were left unsaid.

She never saw my love for what it was. Maybe because I never truly said it, or maybe because she chose not to see it. *I don't know which is worse.*

She would call me in the middle of the night, her voice soft and uncertain.

"Are you awake?"

She always asked, even though she knew I would be. And I always said yes, even when I wasn't.

Sometimes, she talked—about things that didn't seem to matter, about people who had hurt her, about dreams that felt too distant to reach. Other times, she just needed the silence, needed to know that someone was there, that someone cared enough to stay even when there was nothing to say.

And I stayed. *I always stayed.*

But I wonder if she ever knew what those nights meant to me.

To her, I was a safe space—a steady presence she could turn to when she felt lost.

To me, she was everything—the quiet reason even the smallest moments felt meaningful.

I thought, maybe—just maybe—there was something deeper in the way she leaned on me. That the way she reached for me in her moments of doubt meant she felt safe, that she trusted me in ways she didn't trust others. And wasn't that love too?

But love—the kind that changes everything— demands to be named. And we never named it.

We had our moments, though. Moments that made me wonder, that made me hope.

Like that evening on an empty road, the sky bruised with the fading hues of the setting sun. We had been walking for a while, our steps slow, unhurried, as if neither of us wanted to reach the end of the road.

She was quiet, lost in thought, her fingers absentmindedly brushing against the fabric of her jacket. And I was watching her—like I always did—memorizing every little thing.

And then, suddenly, she stopped.

She turned to me, her gaze lingering, searching, as if she was trying to read something in my face.

"You're always there for me," she said softly, almost like a realization.

I swallowed hard, nodding. "Of course I am."

She exhaled, shaking her head slightly. "No, I mean… always."

There was something in her voice, something that made my heart stutter.

And for the first time, I let myself believe.

Maybe she was finally seeing it. Maybe she was finally feeling it too, what had always been right in front of her.

I opened my mouth to say something—to tell her, finally, what I had been too afraid to say for so long.

But before I could, she sighed, a small smile tugging at her lips. "I don't know what I'd do without you."

And just like that, the moment passed.

She wasn't seeing me in a new light. She wasn't realizing anything at all. She was just *grateful*.

Grateful.

She thought my love was kindness. She thought my devotion was just friendship. She thought I was there because I was a good person, not because I was hers in ways she would never be mine.

And it broke me.

Because love should be easy, right? Love should be something you recognize when it's right in front of you. But she never saw it. Or maybe she saw it and didn't want to accept it.

Maybe she didn't want to see it for what it is.

So, I let it be. I let my love remain unspoken, hidden in the spaces between our conversations, in the pauses between her words, in the silence that followed when she finally fell asleep on the phone.

I convinced myself that being there for her was enough. That hearing her voice, even if it was about someone else, was enough. That being the person she turned to, even if she never turned *toward* me, was enough.

But the truth is, love—real love—was never meant to be silent. It was never meant to be something you swallow down and carry like a weight you can't put down.

I started noticing the cracks in my own heart, the little fractures forming every time she told me about someone she liked, every time she leaned on me for support only to walk away without ever truly seeing me.

And still, I stayed. *Because that's what love does, isn't it?* It stays even when it shouldn't.

Then one day, something shifted.

She called, her voice tinged with something different, something heavier. "I feel like I'm losing myself," she whispered.

I wanted to tell her she wasn't lost, that she had always been right here, in my heart. But I couldn't.

Instead, I said, "I'm here."

And that was enough for her. But it wasn't enough for me.

That was the moment I knew—I couldn't keep doing this. I couldn't keep giving pieces of myself to someone who didn't even realize she was holding them.

Maybe love isn't about waiting for someone to see you. Maybe it's about knowing when to walk away.

"Sometimes, love isn't lost—it's just never seen for what it truly is."

CHAPTER 3

ALMOST, BUT NEVER ENOUGH

Love is cruel in the way it tricks you into believing.

It feeds you moments—small, delicate ones—that make you think *maybe*. Maybe this time, maybe this touch, maybe this look means something more. Maybe she's just as lost in you as you are in her.

But love is also cruel in the way it never says it outright. It lets you fill in the blanks, lets you read between the lines, and lets you *hope*.

And hope?

"Hope is the most dangerous thing of all."

I remember the night I almost told her.

It was late—one of those nights where the world felt softer, where silence wrapped around us like a familiar warmth. We were sitting on the hood of my car, parked on an empty road that led to nowhere. The air smelled like rain, the sky stretched endlessly above us, and for a fleeting moment, it felt like we were the only two people in the universe.

She was quiet, staring at the stars, her fingers absentmindedly tracing circles on the cold metal of the car. There was something different about her that night, something almost fragile in the way she held herself. I wanted to ask what she was thinking, but I was afraid to break the moment.

She sighed, her breath visible in the cold air. "Do you ever think about love?"

My heart stilled.

"All the time," I admitted.

She turned to me then, and for a brief second, I thought—*this is it.* This is the moment she finally sees me the way I see her.

But then she smiled, a small, wistful smile, and said, "I wonder what it feels like."

And just like that, I shattered.

She wondered what love felt like.

She had no idea she was sitting next to it.

I gripped the edge of the car, my knuckles white. "You've never been in love before?" I asked, forcing my voice to stay steady.

She shook her head, her gaze drifting back to the sky. "I mean, I've liked people. I've had my moments. But real love? The kind people write songs and poems about?" She let out a soft laugh. "I don't think I've ever felt that."

I looked away, forcing a chuckle of my own. "Yeah. Me neither."

Lies.

I had felt it with every heartbeat since I met her.

I had felt it in the way I noticed every little thing about her—how she chewed on her lip when she was thinking, how she played with the hem of her sleeves when she was nervous, how she laughed with her whole body when something truly made her happy.

I had felt it in the way my heart raced when she got too close, in the way my fingers ached to reach for hers but never did.

I had felt it in the way I memorized all her favorite things, just so I could bring them up at the right moments and watch her face light up.

I had felt it in the way I showed up for her—*always*. No matter what.

And I was feeling it now, as she sat beside me, completely unaware of the fact that she was the very thing she claimed she had never experienced.

"There's nothing more painful than watching someone search for what you've been giving them all along."

That night, I drove her home, listening to her hum softly to a song on the radio, completely unaware of the storm inside me.

She rolled down the window slightly, letting the cold air rush in, her hair dancing with the wind. She looked so at peace, so content. And for a moment, I envied her.

Because for her, this was simple. A quiet night. A drive with a friend.

For me, this was everything. A stolen moment with the person I loved.

As I pulled up in front of her house, she turned to me with that same easy smile, the one that always made me weak.

"Thanks for tonight," she said softly. "I needed this."

I wanted to say something—*anything*. I wanted to tell her that she could have this forever if she only saw me the way I saw her. I wanted to tell her that I loved her, that I had always loved her, that I didn't know how to be anything else but hers.

But all I said was, "Anytime."

She opened the door, hesitated for half a second like she wanted to say something else, then shook her head and stepped out.

And as she walked away without looking back, I knew—I was an *almost.*

Almost hers.

Almost enough.

Almost, but never enough.

And that's the thing about unspoken love. It makes a home in the gaps between what *is* and what *could have been.*

"And sometimes, it stays there forever."

CHAPTER 4

THE LOVE THAT FADED IN SILENCE

Some loves are loud. They exist in grand gestures—declarations shouted across the world, kisses stolen under city lights, fingers intertwined like they were always meant to be.

And then there's the kind of love that stays quiet.

The kind that doesn't demand to be seen. The kind that lingers in late-night conversations, in soft glances across crowded rooms, in the way someone always remembers exactly how you like your coffee. It's the love that stays with you, even when the person doesn't.

That was my love for her.

It was never loud. It never asked for anything.

It just was.

I used to believe love had to be spoken to be real—that if it wasn't declared, confessed, or shouted from rooftops, it didn't count. But with her, I learned that love could exist in silence. That sometimes love isn't in the words you say—it's in the things you do, the moments you share, the spaces between conversations.

And for a long time, I convinced myself that was enough.

Until the night I realized it never would be.

We were at a party, one she had dragged me to, insisting I needed to "get out more." It wasn't my kind of scene—loud music, people I barely knew, the scent of cheap alcohol thick in the air. But she was there, and that was enough of a reason for me to stay.

She was in her element, laughing with effortless ease, dancing with strangers like she belonged to the night itself. She had always been like that—electric, untamed, impossible to hold onto. And yet, I had spent years trying.

At first, I kept my distance, leaning against the wall with a drink in my hand, watching her from across the room.

And then I saw him.

Tall. Confident. The kind of guy who didn't hesitate. He leaned in close, whispered something into her ear, and she laughed—head thrown back, eyes shining.

And then she leaned in too.

Something inside me twisted.

I turned away, gripping the edge of the kitchen counter, trying to breathe past the sudden ache in my chest.

I had no right to be jealous.

She wasn't mine. She had never been mine.

And yet, it felt like I was losing something that had never belonged to me in the first place.

I took a sip of my drink, but it did nothing to dull the sharp edge of reality sinking into my bones. I had spent so long loving her in silence, convincing myself that my presence in her life was enough. That being the one she turned to when she was sad, when she was lost, when she needed comfort—that meant something.

But standing there, watching her melt into the arms of someone who wasn't me, I realized the truth.

I was just a placeholder. A temporary refuge in her storm, a moment of comfort she could always return to—but never stay with. safe space. A convenience. Someone she needed, but never someone she chose.

"Loving someone who doesn't love you back isn't just painful. It's humiliating. Because no matter how much you mean to them, there will always be someone else who means more."

I don't know how long I stood there, staring at nothing, drowning in the kind of heartbreak that doesn't make a sound. The kind that doesn't come with a dramatic ending or a final goodbye. The kind that just is.

But then, I felt a hand on my arm.

"You okay?"

It was her.

Her eyes were slightly unfocused, the alcohol making her movements slower, her words softer. But there was concern in them. Like she knew, somehow, that something was wrong.

And for a second, I almost said it. I almost let the words slip past my lips.

No. I'm not okay. I love you. I love you so much it hurts. I love you in ways you'll never understand. I love you, and I don't know how to stop.

But instead, I forced a smile.

"Yeah," I said. "I'm fine."

She studied me for a moment, like she didn't quite believe me, but then she nodded, giving my arm a small squeeze before disappearing back into the crowd.

And I just stood there, watching her go, feeling the weight of every word I never said.

Because that's the thing about quiet love.

It doesn't leave scars. It doesn't leave bruises.

"It just stays. Unnoticed. Unspoken. Unanswered. And maybe, just maybe, that's the worst kind of love there is."

CHAPTER 5

THE GHOST OF WHAT COULD HAVE BEEN

Loving someone who doesn't love you back doesn't just break you.

It haunts you.

It follows you home at night, slipping between the sheets, filling the spaces they once occupied. It lingers in the songs you used to listen to together, in the inside jokes that no longer make sense to anyone but you, in the scent of their perfume that still clings to your hoodie long after they've left.

It's in the way your heart still jumps when you see their name light up on your phone. In the way you instinctively turn to share something with them before remembering they aren't yours to share things with anymore.

It's in the way every "good morning" and "good night" they once sent feels like a wound that never quite healed.

Because love—real love—doesn't just leave.

It lingers.

And hers had settled into my bones.

I told myself I could move on. That if I ignored the ache long enough, it would fade. That time would do what it always does—soften the edges, blur the details, make it easier to breathe.

But time had passed, and she was still everywhere.

I saw her again a few weeks after that party.

She called me late at night, her voice quieter than usual, like she had been crying or hadn't spoken in hours.

"Can we go for a drive?"

Of course.

It was always **of course** with her.

So I picked her up, like I always did, and we drove without a destination, the city lights blurring past us in streaks of white and yellow. She rolled down the window, letting the cold air rush in, and for a while, we didn't say anything.

She did that sometimes—called me without a reason, asked for my presence without asking for anything else. And I always gave it to her. Because even if she would never be mine, I was still hers in every way that mattered.

Then, out of nowhere, she sighed.

"I think I make people leave," she murmured, her voice barely above a whisper.

I glanced at her, waiting for more.

"Or maybe," she continued, her fingers absentmindedly tracing patterns on the fogged-up window, "I just don't know how to make them stay."

Something about the way she said it made my chest tighten.

She had no idea, did she?

No idea that I had never left. That no matter how many times she had chosen someone else, no matter how many times I had swallowed down my feelings and played the part of the best friend, I had always, always stayed.

I swallowed hard, keeping my voice steady. "You don't have to make the right people stay," I said. "They just do."

She turned her head, her eyes locking onto mine. And for a moment, I thought she saw it—the truth, the love, the years of silent longing trapped inside me.

"You always say the right things," she said softly.

I let out a small, humorless chuckle. "That's because I mean them."

She didn't reply. She just leaned her head against the window, watching the dark sky stretch endlessly above us.

And I wondered, not for the first time, if she had any idea what she meant to me.

"Some people love in loud, obvious ways—kisses, gifts, grand gestures. And then there are people like me, who love in silence, in presence, in staying. And sometimes, that love goes unnoticed. Sometimes, that love isn't enough."

We drove for hours that night.

No destination, no urgency—just two people floating in the quiet between what was and what could never be.

At some point, she fell asleep, her head resting lightly against the car seat, her breathing slow and even.

And I just drove, stealing glances at her every now and then, memorizing the way the passing streetlights cast shadows across her face.

I wanted to tell her then.

That I wasn't like the others. That I wasn't going anywhere. That I had loved her in every way a person could love another—even when it was inconvenient, even when it hurt.

But I didn't.

Because deep down, I knew.

I knew that even if she understood, even if she realized what had been in front of her all along, she still wouldn't have chosen me.

Because some things aren't meant to be.

Some people aren't meant to stay.

Some loves aren't meant to be returned.

I dropped her home that night, like I always did.

And just like always, she walked away without looking back.

And just like always, I sat there for a moment, staring at the empty seat beside me, feeling the weight of every word I never said.

Because that's the thing about unspoken love.

It never really goes away.

It just becomes a ghost that follows you around.

A ghost of almost.

A ghost of what if.

A ghost of something that could have been everything—if only it had been given the chance.

CHAPTER 6

THE WORDS I NEVER SAID

Some nights, I lie awake, staring at the ceiling, replaying every moment I could have said it. Every conversation where my heart screamed the words, but my lips stayed silent. Every time she looked at me like I was her person— the one she could always turn to, the one who understood her without explanation.

I could have told her. I should have told her. But I never did.

Instead, I held it all inside, carrying my love for her like an ocean in my chest—the waves crashing against my ribs, drowning me from the inside out.

The truth is, love doesn't fade just because it's unspoken. It festers. It lingers. It carves itself into every quiet moment, every glance, every missed opportunity.

"Some people think love is loud—grand gestures, passionate confessions. But sometimes, love is the quietest thing in the world. A glance. A hesitation. A word left unsaid."

I remember one night, sitting on my bed, my phone in my hand.

I had written the message so many times before:

I love you. I always have. And I think I always will.

Simple. Honest. Raw.

And yet, my thumb hovered over 'send' as if it were a cliff's edge.

I imagined what would happen next. She would read it. Maybe she'd take a deep breath. Maybe she'd close her eyes for a second. And then she would start typing.

She would say something careful, something soft—something that wouldn't hurt me but wouldn't give me hope either.

"I love you too, but..."

It's the 'but' that would ruin me.

So I deleted the message, turned off my phone, and lay there, letting the silence swallow me whole.

"Some people fear rejection. I feared losing her entirely. So I chose silence—not because I didn't love her enough to confess, but because I loved her too much to risk it."

There were so many moments when I almost said it.

Like the time we were walking home late at night, and she slipped her hand into mine without thinking, just for warmth. I wanted to tell her then.

Like the time she called me at 2 AM, her voice soft, asking, *"Are you awake?"* and I wanted to say, *For you? Always.*

Like the time she leaned her head on my shoulder and sighed, saying, *"I feel safe with you."*

And I wanted to tell her, *You are safe. And you are loved. And you don't even know it.*

But I never did.

Because love, when unspoken, turns into something else.

It turns into weight. It turns into regret. It turns into a thousand moments where you almost say it—but don't.

I wrote her a letter once.

Not one I ever sent, but one I needed to write.

If I told you I loved you, would you stay? Would you look at me the same way? Would we still be us?

Or would you hesitate? Would your eyes search for an answer you don't have? Would you tell me I deserve someone who loves me back the way I need?

I think that's what I'm most afraid of. Not rejection. But the shift. The way things change when truth is spoken out loud. Because once words are said, they can't be taken back. And I can live with loving you in silence. But I don't think I could live with losing you entirely.

I folded the letter, tucked it into a drawer, and let it collect dust—along with every other version of *almost* that we had.

Then one night, I saw her with someone else.

It wasn't unexpected. It wasn't even dramatic.

They were just sitting together, laughing at something, her body turned slightly toward him like she always did when she was interested in someone.

And that was the moment I realized—I had waited too long.

Because love that stays unspoken doesn't wait for you. It moves on. It finds someone who isn't afraid to say it out loud.

And I just sat there, watching, feeling every unsaid word crash over me like a wave I couldn't outrun.

"Maybe love doesn't have to be spoken to be real. But if you keep it locked inside for too long, one day, you'll wake up and realize—what you loved is already gone."

That night, when I got home, I opened my drawer and pulled out the letter.

I read it one last time.

And then I tore it into pieces.

Not because I didn't love her anymore.

But because I knew—some words are meant to stay unsaid.

And maybe, just maybe, this was one of them.

THE SPACE THAT KEPT US APART

Love doesn't vanish overnight. It fades—slowly, painfully, like a song playing on a dying radio, its melody growing quieter until, one day, there's only silence left.

I don't remember exactly when it started happening between us.

Maybe it was when our late-night calls became less frequent, our conversations shorter, the easy flow replaced by awkward pauses. Maybe it was when she stopped sharing the little, insignificant details of her day—the ones she used to tell me with excitement, as if they mattered simply because she was telling me.

Or maybe it was me. Maybe I started pulling back first, without realizing it. Maybe I got tired of waiting for something that was never going to happen.

Either way, the space between us grew.

At first, it was subtle—just a hesitation, a slight pause where there used to be effortless ease. But then, it became something undeniable. A distance neither of us acknowledged, yet both of us felt.

"The worst kind of distance isn't measured in miles. It's in the silence, the hesitation, the invisible walls that grow between two people when love begins to slip away."

I remember the night it hit me.

We were sitting in the same café, in our usual corner, where we had spent countless evenings talking about everything and nothing. But something was different.

She was on her phone more than usual, scrolling through messages, laughing softly at something someone else had sent her. I watched as her fingers danced over the screen—effortlessly, easily—the way they used to when she was texting me.

I wondered who it was.

I didn't ask.

She looked up and smiled, but it wasn't the same. It didn't reach her eyes.

"Sorry," she said, locking her phone and setting it aside. "You were saying something?"

I wasn't. I hadn't spoken in the past five minutes.

And she hadn't noticed.

We used to talk about everything. Now, we only talked about safe things. Surface-level conversations, stripped of depth. No more whispered secrets, no more late-night confessions. Just empty words filling the spaces where something real used to be.

I missed her.

I missed her even when she was sitting right in front of me.

"The loneliest kind of missing isn't when someone is gone. It's when they're still there, but the connection isn't."

One night, I tried to bring it up.

"Do you ever feel like things are changing?" I asked, my voice careful, cautious.

She looked at me, a flicker of confusion in her eyes. "What do you mean?"

I swallowed hard. "Like… I don't know. Like we're not as close as we used to be."

She laughed, but it wasn't the kind of laugh that reassured me.

"You're overthinking," she said, brushing it off. "We're fine."

But we weren't.

And the fact that she didn't see it—or didn't want to—made the space between us even wider.

So I started holding back.

I stopped texting first. Stopped calling as often. Stopped showing up every time she needed me, like I always had.

Not because I wanted to.

But because I needed to know if she'd notice.

If she'd reach out first.

If she'd fight for me the way I had always fought for her.

She didn't.

She still called sometimes, still sent messages, still asked how I was. But the urgency was gone. The need was gone. The us we used to be was gone.

And that's when I knew.

I had been the one holding us together all along.

And now that I had stopped—so had she.

"Maybe that's how you know it was never meant to last—when you stop trying, and it just falls apart on its own."

One day, she mentioned him.

Casually. Like it was nothing. Like it was just another passing detail of her life, as if she hadn't just changed everything in mine.

"There's this guy I've been talking to," she said, stirring her coffee, not meeting my eyes.

I didn't flinch.

Didn't react.

Didn't let her see the way my heart cracked wide open.

"Oh?" I said, forcing a small smile. "Anyone I know?"

She shook her head. "No, just someone I met recently. It's not serious or anything."

Not serious.

Funny how that word stuck with me.

Because for me, everything about her had always been serious.

That night, I went home and sat in the dark for a long time.

I thought about every moment we had shared, every unspoken feeling, every missed opportunity.

I thought about how close we had once been.

And how far apart we were now.

And I realized—the space between us wasn't something that just happened.

It was something I had created.

By waiting too long.

By staying silent.

By choosing my fear over my feelings.

And now, it was too late.

She was slipping away, and I had no one to blame but myself.

"Sometimes, love doesn't die in a single moment. It dies in all the moments you stayed quiet when you should have spoken. In all the times you let the space between you grow, until there was nothing left to hold on to."

CHAPTER 8

LOVING THEM FROM A DISTANCE

There are things in life you can prepare for—heartbreak isn't one of them.

You think you'll handle it. You think you'll be strong. You tell yourself that if it happens, you'll walk away with your head held high, that you'll be happy for them, that you'll let them go with grace.

But then it actually happens.

And you realize—nothing prepares you for watching the person you love, love someone else.

The first time I saw them together, I wasn't expecting it.

I had gone out with some friends, hoping a change of scenery would make things easier. I was laughing at something stupid when I turned my head and—there she was.

With him.

It wasn't anything dramatic.

No stolen kisses. No intertwined fingers. No whispered 'I love yous.'

Just her, standing close to him in a way she never did with me. The way she leaned in when he spoke. The way she smiled without hesitation. The way she looked at him was like he was the only thing in the room.

And in that moment, I knew.

I had lost her.

Not in the way you lose something all at once, like an accident, like a sudden tragedy.

No, this loss had been slow. A quiet unraveling.

And now, I was standing there, looking at the aftermath of my own silence.

"The hardest thing isn't losing them. It's realizing they were never really yours to begin with."

I told myself not to stare.

But my body betrayed me.

My eyes kept searching for details—how close were they standing? Did she laugh differently with him? Was she happier?

It was torture.

And yet, I couldn't look away.

Because in a way, I needed to see it.

I needed proof that she had moved on. That she had found what she was looking for in someone else.

That I had waited too long.

"Some pains demand to be felt. Watching the love of your life fall for someone else is one of them."

My friends must have noticed.

One of them nudged me. "You okay?"

I nodded, forcing a smile. "Yeah, I'm good."

Good.

That was the lie I told myself for weeks.

I was good.

Good at pretending it didn't hurt.

Good at acting like it didn't matter.

Good at convincing myself that I should be happy for her.

Because isn't that what love is supposed to be?

Wanting them to be happy—even if their happiness isn't with you?

But deep down, I wasn't selfless enough for that.

I wanted her happiness.

I just wanted to be the reason for it.

I left early that night.

Reached home.

Instead of going inside, I sat in my car for way too long, staring at the steering wheel, feeling something in my chest that I couldn't name.

It wasn't just heartbreak.

It was grief.

Like mourning something that never even had the chance to live.

"Losing someone hurts. But losing them before you ever really had them? That's a different kind of pain."

I didn't text her for days after that.

Didn't check my phone. Didn't ask her how she was.

And the worst part?

She didn't ask me either.

The space between us had turned into silence.

And silence has a way of confirming what the heart already knows.

She wasn't mine anymore.

She never really had been.

And now, she never would be.

"Maybe love isn't about grand gestures. Maybe it's about timing. And maybe, just maybe—I loved her in every moment, even when life didn't let us align."

CHAPTER 9

MOVING ON (OR AT LEAST TRYING TO)

They say time heals everything.

But they never tell you how much time.

How many mornings you'll wake up with that hollow ache in your chest? How many nights you'll lie in bed, staring at the ceiling, wondering if they ever think of you. How many times you'll hear a song, catch a familiar scent, or pass by a place that makes your heart clench in ways you can't explain.

They just say, Move on.

Like it's a switch you can flip.

Like it's easy.

Like I hadn't spent years loving her in silence.

"Moving on isn't just about forgetting someone. It's about learning to live with the fact that they're happier without you."

I tried everything.

Deleting our old messages.

Changing my lock screen from that blurry photo of us laughing in a café.

Blocking her number—only to unblock it a few days later.

But moving on isn't about erasing someone from your phone.

It's about erasing them from your heart.

And that's the part I kept failing at.

Some nights, I convinced myself I was fine.

I'd go out, meet new people, and let someone make me laugh. And for a moment, I'd think—maybe, just maybe—I was getting over her.

Then I'd see something. Someone ordering her favorite drink. A girl tying her hair up the way she did. A phrase she used to say.

And just like that, I'd be right back where I started.

Because the truth is—love doesn't leave just because you want it to.

"It's easy to walk away from a person. What's hard is walking away from the memories."

I saw her again after a few weeks.

By accident.

Or maybe fate was just cruel.

She was at the bookstore, her fingers grazing the spines of novels, a small smile playing on her lips. She looked… happy. Lighter. Like she had finally let go of something that had been holding her back.

I stood there, frozen.

Should I say something? Should I walk away?

Before I could decide, she turned.

And she saw me.

"Some people are meant to be a lesson. Others are meant to be a memory. And then there are those who are meant to be everything—but never get the chance to be."

"Hey," she said, her voice soft.

It was the same voice I had fallen in love with. The same voice I had memorized like a song.

"Hey," I replied, forcing a smile.

She tilted her head slightly, the way she always did when she was trying to figure out what I was thinking.

"It's been a while."

I nodded. "Yeah."

There was a pause. A familiar kind of silence. The kind we used to be comfortable in. The kind that now felt unbearably heavy.

"How have you been?" she asked.

I wanted to say, *I've been a mess. I've missed you every day. I don't know how to stop loving you.*

Instead, I shrugged. "Good. You?"

She smiled. A real smile. "I'm good too."

And that was it.

That was the moment I realized—she had moved on.

And I was still standing in the same place.

"Moving on isn't when you stop loving them. It's when you accept that they don't love you back."

That night, I went home and did something I had been avoiding for weeks.

I sat down, took a deep breath, and let myself feel everything.

I didn't push it down.

Didn't try to distract myself.

Didn't pretend I was okay.

I just let it hurt.

Because maybe healing wasn't about forcing yourself to move on.

Maybe healing was about sitting with the pain until it no longer controlled you.

Maybe healing was about understanding that some love stories don't end with a period—but with an ellipsis.

A lingering, unfinished thought.

A whisper of what could have been.

"Some wounds don't heal with time. Some wounds heal when you finally allow yourself to feel them."

CHAPTER 10

THE ART OF LETTING GO

Letting go feels like a myth.

People talk about it as if it's a single choice, as if one day, you wake up, take a deep breath, and suddenly, the weight of everything you lost disappears.

But that's not how it works.

Letting go isn't a clean break. It isn't one defining moment. It's a thousand small choices made over and over again.

It's waking up and resisting the urge to check her last seen. It's walking past the café where you used to sit together and not letting it ruin your day. It's hearing her name and not feeling like you've been punched in the stomach. It's unlearning the instinct to reach for your phone whenever something good or bad happens. It's reminding yourself, every damn day, that she's not coming back. And most of all, it's accepting that maybe she was never truly yours to begin with.

"Letting go isn't one big decision. It's a hundred little ones. And some days, you have to make them all over again."

I used to believe that love either lasted forever or faded into nothing.

But what about the love that lingers? The love that stays, even when the person is gone? The love that still whispers to you in quiet moments, making you wonder if they ever think of you too?

That's the hardest kind to let go of.

Because it doesn't just disappear. It stays in your bloodstream. It lingers in your bones. It echoes in your thoughts when you least expect it. And no matter how much you try to drown it out—with distractions, with new people, with long nights spent pretending to be okay—it still finds a way back to you.

"You don't move on all at once. You move on in pieces. And sometimes, the last piece takes the longest to let go."

The truth is, I didn't want to let go. Not really.

Because letting go meant admitting that it was over. That everything we shared—every late-night conversation, every inside joke, every almost-love story—was now just a memory.

And I wasn't ready to turn her into a memory. Because as long as I still held on, as long as a small part of me still hoped, she was still here. Still real. Still mine, in some unspoken way.

But hope is a dangerous thing. Because sometimes, hope is just another way to keep breaking your own heart.

"The hardest part of letting go isn't losing them. It's losing the version of yourself that still believed you had a chance."

I don't know when it started to change. There was no grand moment, no sudden epiphany, no dramatic realization.

It was gradual.

I stopped checking my phone as often. I stopped replaying our conversations in my head. I stopped searching for her face in every crowd. I started focusing on myself—on things I had forgotten I loved. I started reading again, writing again, and going on walks without feeling like I was running from something. I started laughing—not the forced kind, but the kind that comes naturally, effortlessly.

And then, one day, I woke up, and she wasn't the first thought in my mind. That's when I knew—I was healing.

"Maybe letting go isn't about forgetting. Maybe it's about remembering without hurting."

But healing isn't linear. Some days, I still miss her. I still wonder what could have been. There are still moments when I hear a song, see a familiar street, or wake from a dream so vivid that for a moment, it feels like she was just here.

But the difference now? I don't let those moments consume me. I feel them. I acknowledge them. And then, I let them pass.

Because I've learned that letting go isn't about erasing the past. It's about making peace with it.

It's about understanding that some people come into your life not to stay but to teach you something.

And she taught me that love doesn't always mean forever. Sometimes, love just means once.

Once, there was a girl I loved. Once, there was a story we almost wrote together. Once, she meant everything to me.

And now—now, she's just a part of my story. A beautiful, painful, unforgettable part. And that's okay.

"Some people are meant to stay. Others are meant to leave. And then there are the ones who stay with you, even when they're gone."

THE LOVE THAT FOUND ME AGAIN

For the longest time, I believed love was a one-time thing. That you only ever truly fall once, and if it doesn't work out, you're doomed to spend the rest of your life carrying its ghost. That no one else will ever match what you lost. That no one else will ever make you feel the same way.

And maybe that's true. Maybe no one will ever make me feel exactly the way she did. But perhaps that's the point.

Maybe love isn't supposed to feel the same every time. Maybe love isn't about finding a replica of what you lost, but about discovering something new—something unexpected. Something better in ways you never imagined.

And maybe, just maybe, we aren't meant for just one great love in this lifetime.

"The love that breaks you is never the love that saves you. But it teaches you how to recognize the one that will."

The first time I met her, I wasn't looking for love. I wasn't even looking for anything. I had spent so long being trapped in the past that I convinced myself there was no future worth anticipating.

But then—she came along.

Not like a storm, not like a whirlwind. But like a quiet sunrise after a long, sleepless night.

She wasn't loud. She didn't demand my attention. She was just there, in the most effortless way. A presence that didn't overwhelm me but made the silence feel less lonely. A voice that didn't drown out my thoughts but made them softer. A laugh that didn't erase my pain but reminded me that there was still joy in the world.

She never tried to fix me. She never told me to move on, to forget, or to let go faster. She just listened.

And for the first time, I didn't feel the need to hide.

"The right person doesn't heal you. They just remind you that healing is possible."

I told her everything.

About the love I lost. About the girl who still haunted my dreams. About the pain I had carried for far too long.

She didn't flinch. She didn't pull away. She just smiled—a small, knowing smile—and said, "You must have loved her a lot."

I nodded. "Yeah. I did."

She didn't try to compete with that. She didn't try to convince me that what we could have would be better. Instead, she said, "Tell me about her."

And so, I did.

"The right love doesn't erase the past. It just makes it easier to carry."

Loving her was different.

It wasn't an explosion. It wasn't fire. It wasn't something that consumed me entirely.

It was a slow burn. A warmth that grew steadily, without force, without pressure. It was simple moments—laughing over stupid jokes, walking home under city lights, sitting next to each other in comfortable silence. It was late-night conversations that weren't about love but about dreams, fears, and favorite books—the kind of things you only share when you trust someone.

It was peaceful. And maybe that's what I needed.

Not a love that set me on fire. Not a love that felt like a battle I had to win.

But a love that felt like home.

"Some love arrives to teach you lessons. Others arrive to remind you what love is supposed to feel like."

One night, she asked me, "Do you still love her?"

I hesitated. Not because I didn't know the answer, but because I was afraid of it.

Finally, I said, "I think… I will always love her in some way."

She nodded, like she understood. Because she did.

Then she smiled at me and asked, "And do you think… you could love me someday?"

This time, I didn't hesitate.

"I think I already do."

And for the first time in a long time, I wasn't afraid of moving forward.

Because I realized—letting go doesn't mean making room for someone new. It means understanding that love, in all its forms, is infinite. And sometimes, the love that saves you isn't the one that makes your heart race.

It's the one that finally makes it feel at peace.

"The right love doesn't rush you. It waits for you to be ready. And when you are, it's still there."

CHAPTER 12

LOVE, BUT WITHOUT THE HEARTBREAK

Falling in love again felt strange.

Not because I didn't want to—but because, for the longest time, I believed my heart had no room for anyone else.

I had spent so long loving her in silence, so long clinging to the idea that no one could ever replace her, that I failed to realize something important:

"Love isn't something you run out of. It doesn't diminish when given away. It expands. It transforms."

And sometimes, the love you thought was the greatest of your life was merely preparing you for the one that comes after.

Loving her was different.

There weren't the same butterflies. No sleepless nights were spent overanalyzing every word. No heart-stopping moments of uncertainty. And for a while, that terrified me.

Wasn't love supposed to be all-consuming? A wildfire raging through every inch of your soul?

That's how it had felt before.

But maybe—just maybe—love wasn't supposed to hurt. Maybe love wasn't meant to be a battlefield.

With her, there was no guessing. No waiting by the phone, no decoding of mixed signals.

When she liked me, she said it. When she missed me, she told me. When she wanted me close, she reached for me.

And I realized—this is what love is supposed to feel like.

Not a chase. Not a puzzle to solve. But certainty.

"Real love doesn't make you question your worth. It makes you believe in it."

I was used to being the one who loved more. The one who stayed up late, wondering if I crossed their mind. The one who showed up first. The one who cared too much and asked for too little.

But for the first time, I wasn't chasing love. I wasn't begging to be seen. I was standing still. And she came to me—freely, willingly, without hesitation.

There was something profoundly beautiful about that.

I didn't have to fight for her attention. I didn't have to prove I was worthy of love. She just… did.

"The right person doesn't make you earn their love. They give it to you freely—because to them, you're already enough."

One night, as we lay side by side, she asked me, "What was she like?"

I hesitated. Not because I didn't want to talk about her—but because I wasn't sure how to describe a love that once consumed me.

"She was…" I paused, searching for the right words. "She was everything I thought I wanted."

Her fingers brushed softly against mine. "And what am I?"

I turned to meet her gaze, and without thinking, I said,

"You're everything I didn't know I needed."

And it was true.

What I had with her wasn't as intense, but it was real—steady, soft, and sure.

After all the heartbreak, after all the waiting and wondering, maybe this was the love that was meant to stay.

Because the thing about love is—it's never the same twice.

The love that broke me was messy, complicated, and filled with questions I never got answers to. But the love that found me after?

It was quiet. Certain. Whole.

And it didn't demand pieces of me I wasn't ready to give. It didn't ask me to shrink or change. It allowed me to be exactly who I was—flaws, scars, and all.

And for the first time, I realized—maybe love wasn't supposed to hurt. Maybe it was supposed to heal.

"Not every love story is meant to last. But every love shapes you for the one that does."

I still think about her sometimes. Not with longing or regret. But with gratitude.

Because if it weren't for her, I wouldn't have known how deeply I was capable of loving. If it weren't for her, I wouldn't have learned that I deserved to be loved in return.

And if it weren't for her, I might not have recognized the love that finally saved me.

Maybe that's what it means to let go. Not to forget. Not to erase.

But to carry the love forward—without letting it weigh you down.

"Sometimes, the love you lose is just clearing the way for the love that stays."

CHAPTER 13

A LOVE THAT DESERVED TO BE SPOKEN

There are words that stay stuck in your throat—not because you don't want to say them, but because you don't know if they will change anything.

I carried those words for years.

The things I never said. The things I should have said. The things I wanted you to know but was too afraid to speak.

Maybe if I had said them, things would have been different.

Or maybe not.

Maybe some love stories are meant to remain unfinished. But that doesn't mean they didn't deserve to be told.

So this is me, telling ours.

"Some words are too heavy to carry but too painful to let go. So we hold them in, hoping they will fade. But they never do."

I wish I had told you that you were beautiful.

Not in the way people throw the word around like a passing compliment, but in the way I truly saw you.

You were beautiful in the way you laughed when you were nervous. In the way your eyes softened when you spoke about something you loved. In the way you never realized how effortlessly you became my favorite thought, how much space you took in my mind without even trying.

I should have told you that your presence made my world lighter. That every time you walked into a room, the air felt different—like suddenly, it was easier to breathe.

But I never did.

"We assume people know how we feel about them, but they don't. And by the time we're ready to say it, it's too late."

I should have told you that I was scared.

Scared of loving you too much. Scared that one day, you would wake up and decide I wasn't enough.

And maybe that's why I held back.

Maybe that's why I never told you how much I needed you—because needing someone makes you vulnerable, and I didn't want to give you that power.

But you had it anyway.

You had it the moment I looked at you and thought, *She's the one.*

And if I had just said it—if I had just told you everything I felt—would it have changed the way we ended?

Would it have made you stay?

Or were we always meant to be a love that never found its way home?

"The saddest love stories aren't the ones that ended in heartbreak. They're the ones that never got the chance to begin."

I wish I had told you that I understood.

That I knew why you couldn't love me the way I loved you. That I saw the hesitation in your eyes—the way you wanted to hold on but couldn't let yourself.

For so long, I wondered what I did wrong.

But maybe it was never about right or wrong.

Maybe it was about timing.

Maybe it was about the fact that you weren't ready to be loved the way I wanted to love you.

And I can't blame you for that.

"Sometimes, two hearts meet at the wrong time. And no matter how much they want to, they can't beat as one."

I should have told you that I forgave you.

Not because you asked for forgiveness, but because I needed to set myself free from the weight of wanting you to be something you couldn't be

I forgive you for not loving me the way I hoped you would.

I forgive you for choosing distance when I would have chosen closeness.

I forgive you for being the one I couldn't keep.

But most of all, I forgive myself.

For holding on too long. For believing in a future that was never ours. For thinking that love alone would be enough.

Because love *should* be enough.

But not when it's only coming from one side.

"Love isn't about convincing someone to stay. It's about being with someone who chooses to."

If I could go back, would I say all of this to you?

Would I take the chance and tell you everything that was left unsaid?

Maybe.

Or maybe some things are better left as whispers in the past—words written but never spoken, love felt but never returned.

Because at the end of the day, I don't regret loving you.

I don't regret the nights spent thinking of you, the moments where I hoped for something more.

I only regret not telling you that, in every version of my future, you were there.

But maybe now… Maybe it's time to write a future where you are not.

"Closure isn't about getting answers. It's about making peace with the ones you'll never get."

CHAPTER 14

THE LOVE THAT STAYED

Love doesn't always leave.

People do.

Relationships end. Hands let go. Promises fade.

But love? Love stays.

Not always in the way we want it to—not as a presence, not as something we can hold. But as a feeling, a memory, a quiet ache that lingers long after everything else is gone.

And maybe that's what love really is.

Not something that disappears when a person walks away, but something that remains in the way they once made us feel.

"Love doesn't end with goodbye. It lingers in the spaces they once filled, in the echoes of their laughter, in the places where they still exist—even if only in our minds."

I used to believe love was about forever. That if it didn't last, it wasn't real. That if someone left, it meant they never truly cared.

But I was wrong.

Some love stories are brief, yet they are no less meaningful. Some people enter our lives only to leave—but that doesn't mean their love wasn't real.

Love isn't measured by time.

It's measured by the way it changed you.

"Some people love us for a lifetime. Others, for a season. But both leave marks on our hearts that never fade."

She's gone now.

Not in a tragic way, not in a way that demands sadness. Just in the way life pulls people apart, in the way we outgrow the places where we once stood together.

And yet, I still carry her.

Not in my hands, not in my arms. But in my heart.

She is there in the songs I used to play for her. In the way I still pause before saying her name. In the pages of this book, in the words that will always belong to her.

She exists in the smallest details of my days.

In the scent of a perfume that drifts by unexpectedly, one that smells like the way she used to.

In the first sip of coffee in the morning, because she was the one who made me fall in love with its bitterness.

In the way I still type out a message sometimes, only to delete it before sending.

I have let her go.

But I have never erased her.

"Love changes shape, but it never truly leaves. It just finds a new way to exist."

I don't love her the way I used to.

Not with longing. Not with the hope that she will come back.

But with peace. With the quiet understanding that not every love story needs a happy ending to be worth telling.

I loved her. That was enough.

But love didn't leave me empty—it left me open.

I spent so much time believing that letting go was the same as losing. That releasing the weight of unspoken words would somehow erase her importance. But I was wrong. Letting go doesn't mean forgetting; it means accepting that some people are meant to shape us, not stay with us.

And just when I thought my heart had settled into silence, she appeared—the second girl. She didn't arrive with promises of forever or the urgency of filling old voids. She came quietly, without questions or expectations, offering something I hadn't felt in a long time: peace in someone else's presence.

She didn't ask me to forget the past; instead, she helped me understand it. With her, I didn't have to hide the pieces of myself that were still healing. She didn't see me as someone broken by love but as someone learning to carry it differently.

"Not all love stories are written to replace the ones before them—some arrive simply to remind us that it's okay to begin again."

I learned that love can be gentle. It doesn't always come with fireworks or grand gestures. Sometimes, it's in the simplicity of a message that doesn't need to be overthought, a presence that feels like home without trying to be.

And slowly, the pain of the past softened—not because she erased it, but because she stood beside me through it. She became the quiet reminder that I deserved more than lingering goodbyes—I deserved someone who stayed.

I won't call her my happy ending because maybe there's no such thing. But she became something different—my new beginning.

And for the first time, I wasn't holding on to love with trembling hands. I was ready to accept it with open arms.

"Maybe the greatest love stories aren't the ones where everything works out, but the ones where we learn to stay open after the heart has been broken."

You will always be a part of me—the first girl who taught me the depth of unspoken emotions, the weight of silence, and the courage it takes to let go.

Your love stayed—not as a presence, but as a reminder of who I was and who I had to become.

But this chapter isn't just yours anymore.

Because someone else arrived quietly, without demands or promises, and stayed—not as a memory, but as a choice. She became the proof that love isn't always about holding on to what once was; sometimes, it's about making space for what's yet to come.

"Some loves stay in our hearts forever, while others stay by our side—and both are equally real."

So this isn't about the love I lost anymore.

It's about the love I never spoke out loud—and the love I'm finally learning to say.

"The love, left unsaid."

THANKING NOTE

To the one holding this book,

Thank you for picking up these words, for allowing yourself to feel, and for believing that unspoken love matters.

This book wasn't meant to tell a perfect love story—it was meant to tell a true one. If you found yourself in these pages, know you're not alone.

And if this made you think of someone, maybe it's time to say what's been left unsaid.

But remember, love doesn't end in silence. Sometimes, it comes when you least expect it, bringing healing and a new kind of love.

With all my heart,
Avinash Jain

ABOUT THE AUTHOR

Avinash Jain is a writer, poet, and storyteller who found his voice in the spaces between silence and words.

What began as scattered thoughts grew into poems, songs, and stories — each carrying a piece of his heart.

After publishing his first book, he realized that some feelings, even when left unsaid, deserve to be written down.

Love, Left Unsaid is a reflection of that belief — a journey through emotions too deep for conversation but too important to be forgotten.

While Avinash works as a software engineer by profession, his true passion lies in weaving emotions into words.

He dreams big, writes with honesty, and believes that the most beautiful connections are built through stories that feel real.

For those who have loved, lost, hoped, or stayed silent — his writing is a quiet reminder: even the love we leave unsaid leaves a mark that lasts forever.

This is only the beginning of his journey, and he hopes you'll carry a piece of it with you.